# Dinosaur vs.
# BEDTIME

**BOB SHEA**

**Hyperion Books for Children**
**New York**
**An Imprint of Disney Book Group**

For information address Hyperion Books for Children,
114 Fifth Avenue, New York, New York 10011-5690.

First Edition
10 9 8 7 6 5 4 3 2
Printed in Singapore

ISBN 978-1-4231-1335-5
Reinforced binding

Library of Congress Cataloging-in-Publication
Data on file

Visit www.hyperionbooksforchildren.com

**To Ryan,
my little dinosaur**

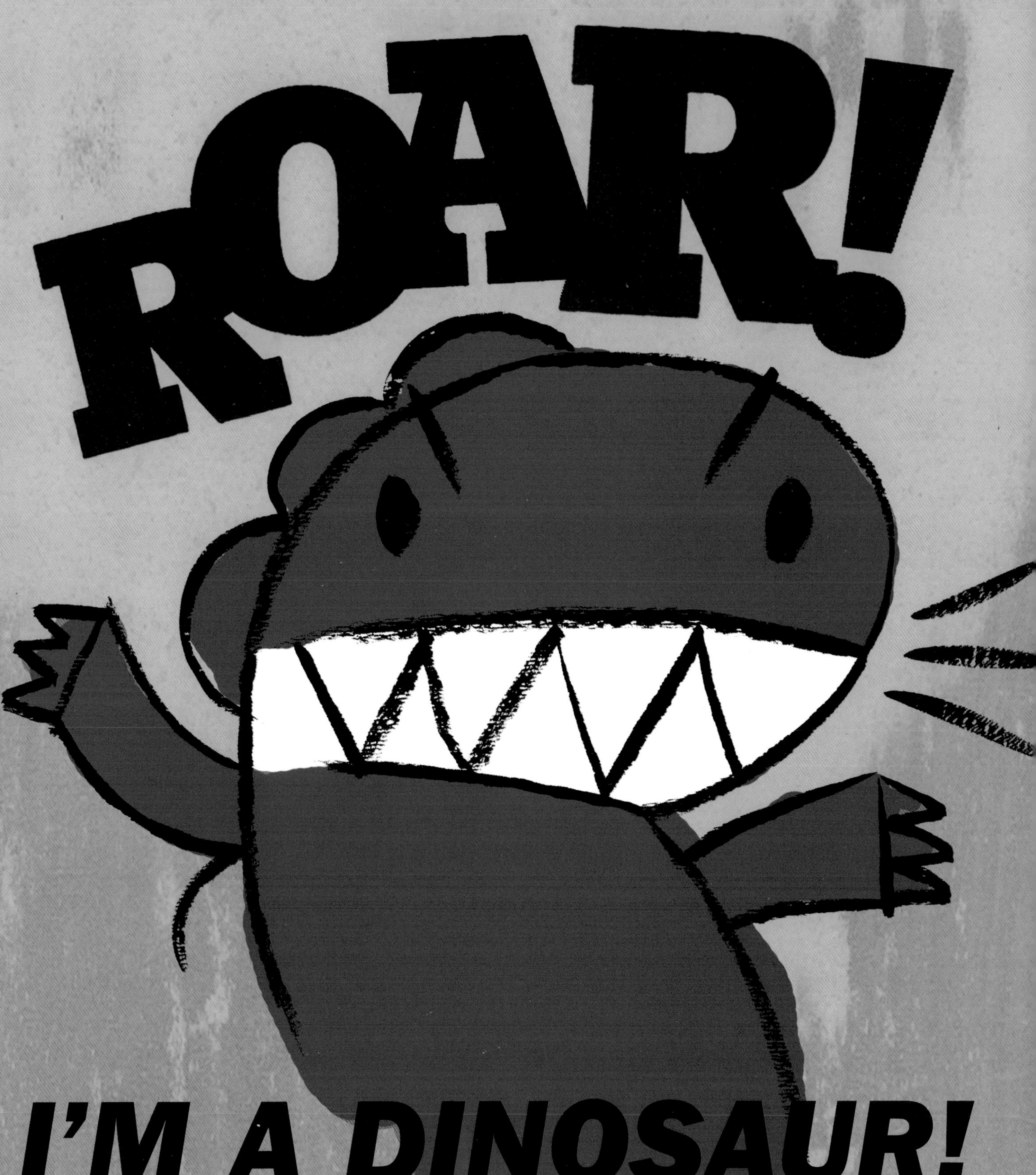


I'M A DINOSAUR!

roar!

roar!

roar!

**Dinosaur versus . . .**

roar! **roar!** roar!

# a PILE OF LEAVES!

# DINOSAUR

# WINS!

roar!

roar!

roar!

**Dinosaur versus . . .**

# DINOSAUR WINS!

roar! roar!
roar!

**Dinosaur versus . . .**

roar!

roar!

# DINOSAUR WINS!

roar!

roar!

roar!

**Dinosaur versus . . .**

# TALKING GROWN-UPS!

roar! roar!

roar!

**Dinosaur versus . . .**

# BATH TIME AND
# TOOTHBRUSHING!

roar!

**roar!**

roar!

roar! **brush! brush! brush!** roar!

# DINOSAUR WINS AGAIN!

roar! roar!

roar!

**Now Dinosaur must face his biggest challenge!**

# BEDTIME!

roar!

roar!

roar!

roar! roar!
roar!

roar!
roar!

roaaar! roaaar!

roaaar! roaaar! roaaaar! rooooar!

# Bedtime wins.

snore
snore
snore

**Good night, dinosaur.**